A Dovetale Press Adaptation
Sherlock Holmes: The Adventure of the Blue Carbuncle
Arthur Conan Doyle

Adapted by Dr Gillian Claridge and Dr B. Sally Rimkeit
Copyright 2016 © Gillian Claridge and B. Sally Rimkeit

All original material in Public Domain. Illustration scans are from Dovetale Press private collections and University of Minnesota Library Collection. Original text from Project Gutenberg.

This edition published by Dovetale Press 2016

Book design by Simon Gotlieb, New Zealand Micrographic Services

Printed by Milne Print, a gold accredited Enviro-Mark NZ, Environmental Management System printer

National Library of New Zealand Cataloguing-in-Publication Data:
Claridge, Gillian.
A Dovetale Press adaptation, Sherlock Holmes,
The adventure of the blue carbuncle Arthur Conan Doyle/
adaptation by Dr Gillian Claridge and Dr B Sally Rimkeit;
original text from Project Gutenberg.
ISBN 978-0-473-37293-4
I. Rimkeit, Sally, 1958- II. Doyle, Arthur Conan,1859-1930.
Adventure of the blue carbuncle. III. Title.
NZ823.3—dc 23

We are grateful for Sponsorship from Bupa

A Dovetale Press Adaptation

Sherlock Holmes:
The Adventure of The Blue Carbuncle

Arthur Conan Doyle

Adaptation by
Dr Gillian Claridge
Dr B. Sally Rimkeit

Illustrations by
Sidney Paget
Frederic Dorr Steele

CONTENTS

CAST OF CHARACTERS

Sherlock Holmes, renowned detective

Dr John Watson, faithful biographer

Mr Peterson, a commissionaire

Mr Henry Baker, a man with a bad hat

The landlord of the Alpha Inn

Mr Breckinridge, a stall holder at Covent Garden

Mrs Maggie Oakshott, who fattens geese for market; she is James Ryder's sister

James Ryder, head attendant at the Hotel Cosmopolitan, and Mrs Oakshott's brother

Mrs Hudson, the landlady at 221B Baker Street.

Chapter 1

The Hat

I called upon my friend Sherlock Holmes on the second morning after Christmas, to wish him the compliments of the season. He was lounging upon the sofa in a purple dressing-gown, and beside him lay a very seedy and disreputable hard-felt hat.

"Do I interrupt you?" I asked.

"Not at all. I am glad to have a friend with whom I can discuss my results. The matter of this hat is a perfectly trivial one, but not entirely devoid of interest."

"I suppose," I remarked, "that, homely as it looks, this thing has some deadly crime linked to it."

"No, no. No crime," said Sherlock Holmes, laughing. "I think this may be perfectly innocent. Do you know Peterson, the commissionaire?"

"Yes. Is it Peterson's hat?" I asked.

Holmes smiled and replied, "No, he found it, and I will tell you how. The owner of the hat is unknown, but it arrived here in the company of a good fat goose.

"The facts are these, Watson: about four o'clock on Christmas morning, the honest Peterson was returning from some small jollification and was making his way homeward down Tottenham Court Road.

"In front of him he saw a tallish man,
carrying a white goose with a black bar
across the tail. As he reached the corner of
Goodge Street, a row broke out between
this stranger and a little knot of roughs.
One of the roughs knocked off the
man's hat, and the man dropped the
goose and ran.

"Peterson had rushed forward to protect the stranger from his assailants, but they all had fled. This left Peterson with this battered hat and a most unimpeachable Christmas goose."

I asked curiously, "Did Peterson return this goose to its owner?"

"My dear fellow, there lies the problem," said Holmes.

"It is true that 'For Mrs Henry Baker' was printed upon a small card which was tied to the goose's left leg, and it is also true that the initials 'H.B.' are legible upon the lining of this hat. But as there are some thousands of Bakers, and some hundreds of Henry Bakers in this city of ours, it is not easy to restore lost property to any one of them."

"What, then, did Peterson do?" I asked.

"He brought round both hat and goose to me on Christmas morning, knowing that even the smallest problems are of interest to me. The goose had to be eaten without delay, so its finder has carried it off to fulfill the ultimate destiny of a goose," said Holmes. "But I continue to retain the hat of the unknown gentleman who lost his Christmas dinner."

"What clue could you have as to his identity?" I asked.

"Only as much as we can deduce from his hat," replied Holmes.

"But you are joking, Holmes," I said. "What can you gather from this old battered felt? I can see nothing."

"On the contrary, Watson," said Holmes, "you can see everything. You fail, however, to reason from what you see.

"The hat's owner is highly intelligent: anyone with a hat of this size must have an unusually large brain capacity.

"The hat is of the best quality, but the style is three years out of date, and it is very worn. Therefore, three years ago, he could afford it. But since he has not replaced it with a new one, he no longer has the means to buy another.

"The owner has, however, endeavoured to conceal some of the stains on the hat by daubing them with ink, which is a sign that he has not entirely lost his self-respect.

"He has greying hair, recently cut, which you can deduce from the hairs adhering to the hat lining. The lining also shows marks of moisture proving that the owner perspired freely, suggesting that he is hardly in the best of training.

"A further point we may deduce from his hat is that his wife has ceased to love him."

"You can tell from the man's hat that his wife has ceased to love him? How is that possible, Holmes?" I asked in amazement.

"This hat has not been brushed for weeks," said Holmes. "When I see you, my dear Watson, with a week's accumulation of dust upon your hat, and when your wife allows you to go out in such a state, I shall fear that you also have been unfortunate enough to lose your wife's affection."

"Well, it is very ingenious," said I laughing. "But since, as you said just now, there has been no crime committed, and no harm done save the loss of a goose, all this seems to be rather a waste of energy."

CHAPTER ONE: THE HAT

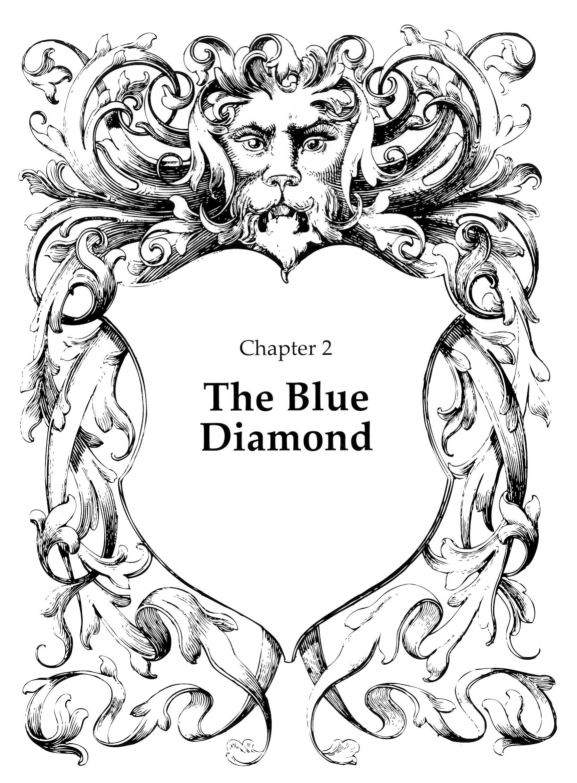

Chapter 2

The Blue Diamond

In the previous chapter …

Sherlock Holmes is presented with a battered hat and Christmas goose when Mr Peterson, the commissionaire, brings them to Holmes on Christmas morning. The commissionaire had stopped some rough young men beating up the owner of the goose and hat, a Henry Baker.

Peterson takes home the goose, which had to be eaten, and Sherlock Holmes keeps the hat. Holmes deduces information from the hat about this Henry Baker, with the view to returning the hat to its rightful owner.

Chapter 2

Sherlock Holmes had just finished explaining to me the matter of the goose, when the door flew open. Peterson, the commissionaire, rushed into the apartment with flushed cheeks and the face of a man who is dazed with astonishment.

"The goose, Mr Holmes! The goose, sir!" Peterson gasped.

"Eh? What of it, then? Has the goose returned to life and flapped off through the kitchen window?" Holmes asked.

"See here, sir! See what my wife found in its crop!" cried Peterson.

He held out his hand and displayed upon the centre of the palm a brilliantly scintillating blue stone. It was rather smaller than a bean in size, but of such purity and radiance that it twinkled like an electric point in the dark hollow of his hand.

"A diamond, Mr Holmes? A precious stone. It cuts into glass as though it were putty."

Holmes looked at the blue stone.
"It's more than a precious stone. It is the Countess of Morcar's blue carbuncle!" Holmes exclaimed. "This blue diamond was stolen from the Hotel Cosmopolitan five days ago, and there is a thousand pound reward for its return."

"A thousand pounds! Great Lord of mercy!" Peterson plumped down into a chair and stared from one to the other of us.

"A thousand pounds is probably not a twentieth fraction of the blue carbuncle's value on the open market," continued Holmes.

Holmes read from the newspaper: "'John Horner, a plumber, was accused of the theft of the valuable gem known as the blue carbuncle, which he took from the jewel-case of the Countess of Morcar.

"'James Ryder, upper-attendant at the hotel, said in his evidence that he had shown Horner up to the dressing-room of the Countess of Morcar upon the day of the robbery. Horner was to solder a pipe which was leaking.

"'When James Ryder returned later, he found that Horner had disappeared. A dressing-table drawer had been forced open. The jewel-case in which the Countess usually kept the blue carbuncle was lying empty upon the dressing-table.

"'Ryder instantly gave the alarm, and Horner was arrested the same evening; but the carbuncle could not be found.

"'Catherine Cusack, maid to the Countess, agreed with Ryder's testimony. Horner, however, protested his innocence.'

"Hum!" said Holmes thoughtfully, "You see, Watson, our little deductions have suddenly assumed a much more important and less innocent aspect.

"Here is the blue carbuncle. The blue carbuncle came from the goose, and the goose came from Mr Henry Baker, the gentleman with the bad hat.

"So now we must set ourselves very seriously to finding Mr Henry Baker and ascertaining what part he has played in this little mystery," said Holmes.

"How will you do that?" I asked.

Holmes said, "We will put the following advertisement in the evening papers: 'Found at the corner of Goodge Street, a goose and a black felt hat. Mr Henry Baker can have the same by applying at 6:30 this evening at 221B Baker Street.'

CHAPTER TWO: THE BLUE DIAMOND

"That is clear and concise," Holmes continued, "Now, Peterson, will you take the advertisement to the newspapers. And on your way back be so good as to purchase a goose of the same size and weight as the one you and your family have just consumed."

Mr Peterson left to take the advertisement to the newspapers.

Holmes picked up the blue carbuncle and held it against the light.

"It's a bonny thing," he said. "Just see how it glints and sparkles. Of course it is a nucleus and focus of crime. Every good stone is. They are the devil's pet baits.

"This stone is not yet twenty years old but it has already a sinister history. There have been two murders, a vitriol-throwing, a suicide, and several robberies brought about for the sake of this forty-grain weight of crystallised charcoal, this blue carbuncle.

"I will inform its owner, the Countess of Morcar, that we have it," Holmes concluded.

"Do you think that Henry Baker had anything to do with the robbery?" I asked.

"I shall determine that by a very simple test, if we have an answer to our advertisement," said Holmes.

"In that case, I shall return at half past six to see what has transpired," I said.

CHAPTER TWO: THE BLUE DIAMOND

Chapter 3

Mr Baker

In the previous chapter ...

Mr Peterson tells Sherlock Holmes and Dr Watson that he has just found the famous blue carbuncle, a very valuable diamond, in the gullet of the goose. The diamond was recently stolen from a London hotel.

A plumber has been accused of the theft, but he says he is innocent. Sherlock Holmes advertises the finding of the goose and hat in the hope that the owner will reveal how he got the goose, and whether he has any knowledge of the diamond inside it.

———————

Chapter 3

I returned to Holmes' apartment shortly after half past six. I saw there a tall man in a Scotch bonnet, his coat buttoned up to his chin, who had also just arrived. Holmes greeted this visitor with an easy air of geniality.

"Pray take this chair by the fire, Mr Baker. It is a cold night, and I observe that your circulation is more adapted for summer than for winter. Ah, Watson, you have come just at the right time.

"Is that your hat, Mr Baker?" asked Holmes.

"Yes, sir, that is undoubtedly my hat."

Mr Henry Baker was a large man with rounded shoulders and a massive head. He had a broad, intelligent face, sloping down to a pointed beard of grizzled brown.

Mr Baker's rusty black frock-coat was buttoned right up in front. His lank wrists protruded from his sleeves without a sign of cuff.

CHAPTER THREE: MR BAKER

Mr Baker spoke slowly, choosing his words with care. He gave the impression of a man of learning and letters who had had ill-usage at the hand of fortune.

"We can return your hat, sir," said Holmes to Mr Baker, "but as for your goose, we were compelled to eat it."

"To eat it!" Henry Baker half rose from his chair in his excitement.

"Yes, it would have been of no use to anyone had we not done so. But I presume that this other goose upon the sideboard, which is about the same weight and perfectly fresh, will answer your purpose equally well?"

"Oh, certainly, certainly," answered Mr Baker with a sigh of relief.

"Of course, we still have the feathers, legs, crop, and so on of your own bird, so if you wish—"

Mr Baker burst into a hearty laugh.
"They might remind me of my adventure,"
said he, "but beyond that I can hardly see
what use they would be to me!"

Sherlock Holmes glanced sharply across at
me with a slight shrug of his shoulders.
"There is your hat, then, and there your
goose," he said to Mr Baker.

"By the way, would it bore you to tell me
where you got the other one from?"
continued Holmes, "I am somewhat of a
fowl fancier, and I have seldom seen a
better grown goose."

"Certainly, sir," said Baker, who had risen
and tucked the fresh goose under his arm.
"There are a few of us who drink at the
Alpha Inn, near the British Museum.
This year we instituted a goose club.
By paying a few pence every week, we
were each to receive a goose at Christmas.

"My pence were duly paid, and as you know, I was attacked on the way home with the goose; I thought the assailants had taken both my hat and the goose. I am much indebted to you, sir, for returning both."

Mr Baker bowed solemnly to both of us and strode off upon his way.

"So much for Mr Henry Baker," said Holmes when he had closed the door behind him. "It is quite certain that he knows nothing whatever about the matter.

"Watson, if you do not require dinner immediately, I suggest that we go to the Alpha Inn now and discover the provenance of the goose."

"By all means," I said.

CHAPTER THREE: MR BAKER

Chapter 4

The Goose Chase

In the previous chapter…

A Mr Henry Baker comes to Sherlock Holmes' apartment to claim his hat and goose.

He knows nothing of the diamond, but tells Holmes that he got it through a Christmas Club set up in the Alpha Inn near the British Museum.

Holmes and Watson therefore set out to the Alpha Inn to find out more about the goose.

———————

Chapter 4

It was a bitter night, so Holmes and I drew on our ulsters and wrapped cravats about our throats. Outside, the stars were shining coldly in a cloudless sky.
The breath of the passers-by blew out into smoke like so many pistol shots.

In a quarter of an hour we were at the Alpha Inn. Holmes pushed open the door of the private bar and ordered two glasses of beer from the ruddy-faced, white-aproned landlord.

"Your beer should be excellent if it is as good as your geese," Mr Holmes said.

"My geese!" The landlord seemed surprised.

"Yes. I was speaking only half an hour ago to Mr Henry Baker, who was a member of your goose club."

"Ah! yes, I see. But you see, sir, them's not our geese. I got the two dozen from a salesman called Breckinridge in Covent Garden." said the landlord.

"Ah! Thank you, landlord," said Holmes.

We drank our beer and set off to Covent Garden, to find Mr Breckinridge.

As we walked, Holmes remarked, "The conundrum of the blue carbuncle inside the goose may seem trivial, but Mr Horner, the man accused of stealing the blue carbuncle, could face seven years of penal servitude if he is convicted. It is by no means certain that he was the thief.

"Our inquiry may only confirm Horner's guilt but it may establish his innocence. So quick march to Covent Garden, Watson!"

At Covent Garden we swiftly found Mr Breckinridge's stall, where he was just shutting up for the night. "Good evening," said Holmes. "You are sold out of geese, I see?"

"Let you have five hundred to-morrow morning," said Mr Breckinridge.

"But I need one now. Where did you get your fine birds from?" Holmes said.

"Why all these questions about the geese all of a sudden?" asked Mr Breckinridge angrily.

His angry reaction to Holmes' enquiries about the goose surprised me.

He continued, "I've paid good money for those geese, they are good quality geese. I'm tired of people asking me about them.

"If you've got any questions about the quality of my geese, go to Mrs Oakshott, 117 Brixton Road and ask her," said Mr Breckinridge. "She supplied them!"

Chapter 5

The Thief

In the previous chapter...

Sherlock Holmes and Dr Watson go to the Alpha Inn. The landlord explains that when the Christmas Club members give him money collected over the year, he buys them each a goose from a Mr Breckinridge of Covent Garden.

When Holmes and Watson find Mr Breckinridge, he tells them that the goose came from a Mrs Oakshott of Brixton Road, who fattens geese for Christmas. Another person has also been questioning Mr Breckinridge about the goose.

Chapter 5

Holmes and I had only just walked away from Mr Breckinridge's stall when we heard a hubbub breaking out there. Looking round, we saw a little rat-faced fellow standing in front of Breckinridge, who was shaking his fists fiercely at the cringing figure.

"I've had enough of you and your geese," shouted Breckinridge. "You bring Mrs Oakshott here and I'll answer her, but what have you to do with it? Did I buy the geese off you?"

"No. But one of them was mine all the same," whined the little man.

Breckinridge raised his fist threateningly, and the little man hastily flitted away into the darkness.

"Ha! This may save us a visit to Mrs Oakshott," whispered Holmes. "Come with me, Watson, and we will see what is to be made of this fellow."

Holmes speedily overtook the little man and touched him upon the shoulder. He sprang round, and every vestige of colour drained from his face.

"Who are you, then? What do you want?" the little man asked in a quavering voice.

"You will excuse me," said Holmes blandly, "but I think that I could be of assistance to you. You are endeavouring to trace some geese which were sold by Mrs Oakshott of Brixton Road."

"You? Who are you? How could you know anything of the matter?" cried the little man.

"My name is Sherlock Holmes. It is my business to know what other people don't know."

"Oh, sir," cried the little fellow with out-stretched hands and quivering fingers. "I can hardly explain to you how interested I am in this matter."

Sherlock Holmes hailed a cab, which was passing. "In that case let us discuss it in the comfort of my rooms," said he. "But pray tell me, before we go farther, who it is that I have the pleasure of assisting,"

The man hesitated for an instant. "My name is James Ryder."

"Precisely so," said Sherlock Holmes. "You, Mr Ryder, are the head attendant at the Hotel Cosmopolitan. Pray step into the cab, and I shall soon be able to tell you everything which you would wish to know."

Ryder stood glancing from one to the other of us with half-frightened, half-hopeful eyes, as one who is not sure whether he is on the verge of a windfall or of a catastrophe.

Then Ryder stepped into the cab, and in half an hour we were back in the sitting-room at Baker Street.

"Here we are!" said Holmes cheerily as we filed into the room. "The fire looks very seasonable in this weather. You look cold, Mr Ryder. Pray take the basket-chair. I will just put on my slippers before we settle this little matter of yours.

"Now, then! You want to know what became of those geese?" asked Holmes.

"Yes, sir," replied James Ryder.

"Or rather, I fancy, of that goose," said Holmes. "It was one bird, I imagine in which you were interested— white, with a black bar across the tail."

Ryder quivered with emotion. "Oh, sir," he cried, "can you tell me where it went to?"

"It came here," said Holmes.

"Here?" said Ryder.

"Yes, and a most remarkable bird it proved. It laid an egg after it was dead— the bonniest, brightest little blue egg that ever was seen. I have it here in my museum," Holmes replied.

CHAPTER FIVE: THE THIEF

James Ryder staggered to his feet. Holmes unlocked his strong-box and held up the blue carbuncle, which shone out like a star, with a cold, brilliant, many-pointed radiance.

Ryder stood glaring, uncertain whether to claim or to disown it.

"The game's up, Ryder," said Holmes quietly. "Help him back into his chair, Watson. Give him a dash of brandy. So! Now he looks a little more human. What a shrimp he is, to be sure!"

For a moment Mr Ryder had nearly fallen, but the brandy brought a tinge of colour into his cheeks, and he sat staring with frightened eyes at his accuser.

Chapter 6

The Season of Forgiveness

In the previous chapter…

When Holmes and Watson leave Mr Breckinridge, they see a little rat-faced man speaking to him and having an argument about the goose. Holmes quickly offers to help the little man find the goose, and takes him to his apartment. The man's name is James Ryder and he is the head attendant at the Cosmopolitan Hotel, from where the blue diamond was stolen.

Holmes realises that Mr Ryder is the thief, and that he has contrived the evidence so that Mr Horner the plumber was accused. Holmes shows Ryder the diamond and Ryder understands that the game is up.

Chapter 6

"How did you hear of the Countess of Morcar's blue carbuncle?" Sherlock Holmes asked James Ryder.

"It was Catherine Cusack who told me of it, her ladyship's waiting-maid," said Mr Ryder in a crackling voice.

"Well, Ryder," said Holmes, "It seems to me that you have the making of a very pretty villain in you.

"In order to throw suspicion on Horner the plumber you invented some small job for him in her ladyship's room.
Then, when he had left, you rifled the jewel-case, raised the alarm, and had the unfortunate Horner arrested. You then—" said Holmes.

Ryder threw himself down suddenly upon the rug and clutched at Holmes' knees.

"For God's sake, have mercy!" Ryder
shrieked. "Think of my father! Of my
mother! It would break their hearts.
I never went wrong before! I never
will again. I'll swear it on a Bible.
Oh, don't bring it into court!
For Christ's sake, don't!"

"It is very well to cringe and crawl now,"
said Holmes sternly, "but you thought little
enough of putting poor Horner the
plumber in the dock for a crime of which
he knew nothing.

"And now let us hear how the blue
carbuncle came into the goose?
Tell us the truth, for there lies your
only hope of safety."

Ryder passed his tongue over his parched
lips. "I will tell you just as it happened,
sir," said he.

"When Horner had been arrested, I was
afraid the police would search me and my
room, so I went to my sister's house. She is
Mrs Oakshott, and lives on Brixton Road,
and she fattens fowls for the market.

"When I got to my sister's house, I went into the backyard to smoke a pipe, and wondered what to do with the blue carbuncle.

"I remembered an old friend of mine, Maudsley, who is a thief, and has just come out of jail. I thought he might be able to sell the blue carbuncle for me, but how to get it to him? Then I saw the geese, and an idea came into my head which showed me how I could beat the best detective that ever lived.

"My sister had offered me a goose for Christmas, so I caught one of the birds—a fine big goose, white, with a barred tail. Prying its bill open, I thrust the stone down its throat.

"When I forced the blue carbuncle into the goose's beak, it gave a gulp. I felt the stone pass along its gullet and down into its crop," continued Ryder.

"Just then, my sister appeared and startled the goose, which flapped away to the rest of the flock. I told my sister I wanted the white goose with the barred tail, so she told me to kill it and take it away with me. I did so, and took it to my friend Maudsley, the thief.

"But when I got to Maudsley's house, and we opened up the goose, there was no sign of the stone, and I knew that some terrible mistake had occurred.

"I left the bird, rushed back to my sister's, and hurried into the back yard. There was not a bird to be seen there.

"'Where are they all, Maggie?' I cried," continued Ryder.

"'Gone to the dealer's, to Breckinridge of Covent Garden,' said Maggie.

"'But was there another with a barred tail?' I asked, "'the same as the one I chose?'

"'Yes, Jem. There were two barred-tailed ones, and I could never tell them apart,' said my sister.

"Well, then, of course I saw it all," said Ryder, "It was the second bar-tailed goose that had swallowed the blue carbuncle. I ran off as hard as my feet would carry me to this man Breckinridge to find it. But he had sold all the geese at once and would not tell me where they had gone.

"My sister thinks that I am going mad. Sometimes I think that I am myself. And now— and now I am myself a branded thief, without ever having touched the wealth for which I sold my character.

"God help me! God help me!" James Ryder burst into convulsive sobbing, with his face buried in his hands.

CHAPTER SIX: THE SEASON OF FORGIVENESS

There was a long silence. Then Sherlock Holmes rose and threw open the door. "Get out!" said he.

"What, sir! Oh, Heaven bless you!" cried Ryder.

"No more words. Get out!"

And no more words were needed. The door banged and we heard the rattle of Ryder's running footfalls from the street.

"After all, Watson," said Holmes, "I am not answerable to the police. If Horner were in danger it would be another thing; but James Ryder will not appear against him, and the case must collapse.

"I suppose that I am commuting a felony, but it is just possible that I am saving a soul. Ryder will not go wrong again. He is too terribly frightened. Send him to jail now, and you make him a jailbird for life.

"Besides, it is the season of forgiveness. Chance has put in our way a most singular and whimsical problem, and its solution is its own reward," and Holmes reached up his hand to take his clay pipe.

"And now," Holmes continued, "If you will have the goodness to touch the bell, Doctor, we will begin another investigation, in which a bird will also be the chief feature, for I understand that the good Mrs Hudson has ready a woodcock for our dinner."

I did as he asked, and we dined heartily on the aforementioned bird.

CHAPTER SIX: THE SEASON OF FORGIVENESS

Profits from this
edition support our
international reading
and dementia study.